HELLO,
I AM CHARLIE!
from London

Hello, I am Charlie from London! Come inside to meet my family and my friends...

Stéphane Husar
Illustrated by Yannick Robert

FICTION READALONG
AV2 BY WEIGL
ADDED VALUE • AUDIO VISUAL

www.av2books.com

Your AV² Media Enhanced book gives you a fiction readalong online. Log on to www.av2books.com and enter the unique book code from page 2 to use your readalong.

AV² Readalong Navigation

HIGHLIGHTED TEXT

HOME 🏠

CLOSE ⊗

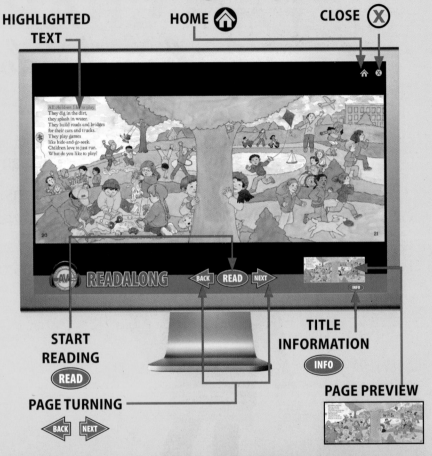

START READING
READ

PAGE TURNING
BACK NEXT

TITLE INFORMATION
INFO

PAGE PREVIEW

Go to **www.av2books.com**, and enter this book's unique code.

BOOK CODE

R 1 3 4 5 6 4

AV² by Weigl brings you media enhanced books that support active learning.

First Published by

Published by AV² by Weigl
350 5ᵗʰ Avenue, 59ᵗʰ Floor New York, NY 10118
Websites: www.av2books.com   www.weigl.com

Printed in the United States of America in North Mankato, Minnesota
1 2 3 4 5 6 7 8 9 0 18 17 16 15 14

042014
WEP080414

Library of Congress Control Number: 2014937140

ISBN 978-1-4896-2256-3 (hardcover)
ISBN 978-1-4896-2257-0 (single user eBook)
ISBN 978-1-4896-2258-7 (multi-user eBook)

Text copyright ©2009 by ABC MELODY.
Illustrations copyright ©2009 by ABC MELODY.
Published in 2009 by ABC MELODY.

ABC MELODY Éditions
26, rue Liancourt 75014
Paris, France

Contents

My name is Charlie.
I am eight years old.
I live in London, the capital of England.
London is a big city with double-decker buses
and black cabs everywhere.
How many buses do you see on this page?

4

a city

a cab

a bus

England

5

In London, we have the biggest clock in the world.
It is called Big Ben.
What time is it now?

Big Ben

a clock

What time is it?

big / small

In England, we have a queen. She lives in a big house called Buckingham Palace.
It has more than six hundred rooms.
Wow! She must have a big family!

8

a queen

Buckingham Palace

a room

a family

I live with my family in a pretty house with a pretty garden.
I have one little brother and one big sister, a cat and a rabbit.
I don't know where they are. Can you find them?

a house

a garden

my sister

my brother

my rabbit

My mom is a florist. She loves flowers.
My dad is a fireman. He drives a big fire engine.
One day, I want to be a fireman, too!

my mom

my dad

a flower

a fireman

a fire engine

Here is Henry, my cat. He sleeps all day and goes out all night. We don't know where he goes, but he is always tired in the morning.

my cat

to sleep

the night

the morning

tired

This is my school. I have a lot of friends there: James, Abdul, Niki and Stella. They all come from different countries. I like Stella a lot. She is very clever and very pretty.

my school

my friends

pretty

clever

At school, we learn French. This is great because in my class, there is a French boy called Pierre.
I can speak French to him.

Salut Pierre, ça va ?

18

my class

a girl

a boy

French

19

I like to play football with my friends.
On Sundays, I ride my bike in Hyde Park with
Dad. Henry stays at home. He doesn't ride bikes.
He prefers to watch TV.

20

to play football

to ride a bike

to watch TV

a park

We love music in my family.

My mom sings. I play the saxophone. My sister plays the trumpet.

My brother plays the tambourine. Henry plays the piano.

And my father dances.

to sing

to play the saxophone

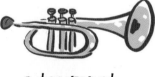

a trumpet

a piano

23

In England, we drink a lot of tea.
My favorite meal is breakfast. I have cornflakes,
jam and toast, and a large orange juice.
It's delicious!

cornflakes

jam and toast

orange juice

tea

25

In the summer, we drive up to Blackpool.
Blackpool is in the north of England.
No, this is not the Eiffel Tower! It is the Blackpool Tower.
I love the beach, but the water is very cold at Blackpool.

summer

the beach

water

cold

At Christmas, we all go to York to see my grandfather and my grandmother. They live in the countryside. We decorate the house and we get a lot of great presents!

Christmas

my grandmother

my grandfather

a present

29

That's it! The visit is over!
I hope to see you soon in London. Goodbye!

Bye!

Bye bye!

Goodbye!